THE
GREAT
BLUENESS
and
OTHER
PREDICAMENTS

by

ARNOLD LOBEL

HARPER & ROW, PUBLISHERS
NEW YORK, EVANSTON, AND LONDON

Remembering Patrick

Long ago there were no colors in the world at all.
Almost everything was grey,
and what was not grey was black or white.
It was a time that was called The Great Greyness.

Every morning a Wizard who lived
during the time of The Great Greyness
would open his window to look out at the wide land.
"Something is very wrong with the world," he would say.
"It is hard to tell when the rainy days stop
and the sunny days begin."

The Wizard would often
go down the stairs
to his dark, grey cellar.

There, just to amuse himself
and to forget about
the drab world outside,
he would make
wonderful magic potions and spells.

One day while the Wizard was mixing and stirring
a little of this and a bit of that,
he saw something strange in the bottom of his pot.
"What good-looking stuff I have made!" he exclaimed.
"I will make some more right away."

"What is it?" asked the neighbors
when they saw the Wizard painting his house.
"A color," said the Wizard. "I call it *blue*."
"Please," cried the neighbors, "please give us some!"
"Of course," said the Wizard.

And that was how The Great Blueness came to be.

After a short time everything in the world was blue.

Trees were blue. Bees were blue.

Wheels and evening meals were blue.

The Wizard would pedal out on his blue bicycle

to look around at the wide, blue world.

He would say, "What a perfect day we are having."

But The Blueness was not so perfect.
After a long time all that blue
made everyone sad.
Children played no games.
They sulked in their blue backyards.
Mothers and fathers sat at home
and stared gloomily
at the blue pictures on the walls
of their blue living rooms.
"This Blueness is too depressing,"
said the neighbors to the Wizard,
who was unhappier than anyone.
"Nobody laughs anymore," he said.
"Even I myself have not smiled for days."

"I must do something," said the Wizard
as he slouched down the stairs
to his dark, blue cellar.

There he began to mix and stir
a little of this and a bit of that.
Soon he saw something new
in the bottom of his pot.
"Now here is happier stuff," said the Wizard.
"I will make some more right away."

"What is that?" asked the neighbors
when they saw the Wizard painting his fence.
"I am calling it *yellow*," said the Wizard.
"May we have some?" begged the neighbors.
"You may," replied the Wizard.

And that was how The Great Yellowness came to be.

After a short time everything in the world was yellow.

There was not a flyspeck of blue anywhere to be seen.

Pigs were yellow.   Wigs were yellow.

Stairs and dentist chairs were yellow.

The Wizard would gallop out on his yellow horse
to explore the wide, yellow world.

He would say, "What a fine day we are having."

But The Yellowness was not so fine.
After a long time all that yellow
began to hurt everyone's eyes.
People walked about
bumping and thumping into each other.
They were squinting
and could not see where they were going.
"This Yellowness is too bright and blinding,"
said the neighbors to the Wizard.
"You don't have to tell me," moaned the Wizard,
who had a cold towel on his head.
"Everyone has a headache, and so do I."

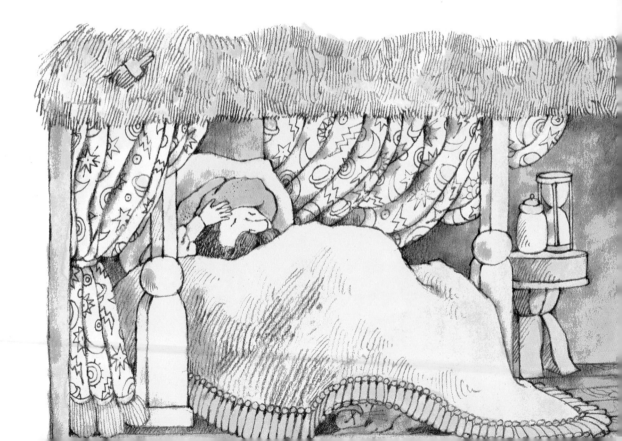

So the Wizard stumbled
down the stairs
to his dark, yellow cellar.

There he mixed and stirred
a little of this
and a bit of that.
Soon he saw something different
in the bottom of his pot.
"This is handsome stuff," declared the Wizard.
"I will make some more right away."

"What do you call that?" asked the neighbors
when they saw the Wizard painting his flowers.
"*Red,*" answered the Wizard.
"We would like some too," pleaded the neighbors.
"Right away," said the Wizard.

And that was how The Great Redness came to be.

After a short time everything in the world was red.

Mountains were red. Fountains were red.

Limburger cheese and afternoon teas were red.

The Wizard would sail out in his red boat

to see what he could see of the wide, red world.

He would say, "What a glorious day we are having."

But The Redness was not so glorious.
After a long time all that red
put everyone into a very bad temper.
Children spent their days fighting
and punching each other
while mothers and fathers argued loudly.
A furious crowd of neighbors
marched to the Wizard's house.
"This awful Redness is all your fault," they shouted.
Then they threw stones at the Wizard,
who jumped up and down and gnashed his teeth
because he was in such a terrible temper himself.

The Wizard stormed
down the stairs
to his dark, red cellar.

He mixed and stirred for many days.
He used all the magic that he could think of
to find a new color, but all that he made
was more and more blue,
more and more yellow,
and more and more red.
The Wizard worked until all of his pots
were filled to the top.

But The Redness was not so glorious.
After a long time all that red
put everyone into a very bad temper.
Children spent their days fighting
and punching each other
while mothers and fathers argued loudly.
A furious crowd of neighbors
marched to the Wizard's house.
"This awful Redness is all your fault," they shouted.
Then they threw stones at the Wizard,
who jumped up and down and gnashed his teeth
because he was in such a terrible temper himself.

The Wizard stormed
down the stairs
to his dark, red cellar.

He mixed and stirred for many days.
He used all the magic that he could think of
to find a new color, but all that he made
was more and more blue,
more and more yellow,
and more and more red.
The Wizard worked until all of his pots
were filled to the top.

The pots were so full that they soon overflowed.
The blue and the yellow and the red
all began to mix together.
It was a terrible mess.
But when the Wizard saw what was happening,
he exclaimed, "That is the answer!"
And he danced joyfully around the cellar.

The Wizard mixed
the red with the blue
and made a new color.

The Wizard mixed
the yellow with the blue
and made a new color.

The Wizard mixed
the yellow with the red
and made a new color.
"Hurrah!" he shouted, and he mixed
the red and the blue and the yellow
in all kinds of different ways.

"Look at these beautiful things I have made!"
said the Wizard when he was finished.
"What are they?" asked the neighbors.
"I call them purple and green and orange and brown,"
said the Wizard.
"They are a sight for sore eyes," cried the neighbors,
"but which one shall we choose this time?"
"You must take them all," said the Wizard.

The people did take all the colors the Wizard had made.
After a short time they found good places for each one.
And after a long time when the Wizard opened his window,
he would look out and say,
"What a perfectly fine and glorious day we are having!"

The neighbors brought the Wizard gifts
of red apples and green leaves
and yellow bananas and purple grapes
and blue flowers.
At last the world was too beautiful
ever to be changed again.